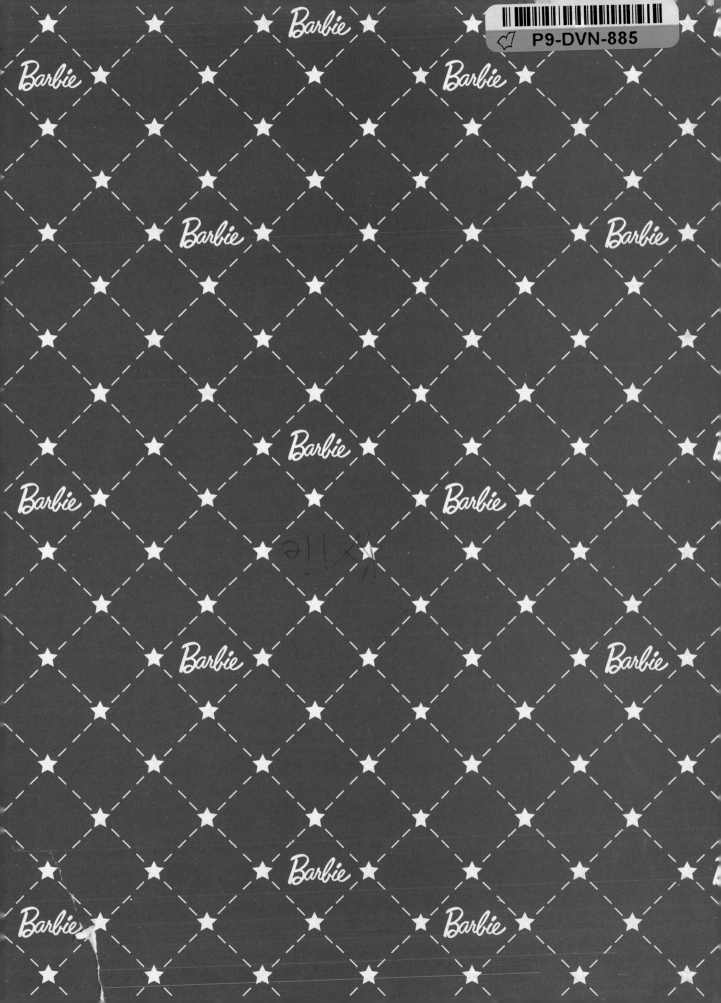

Kylie

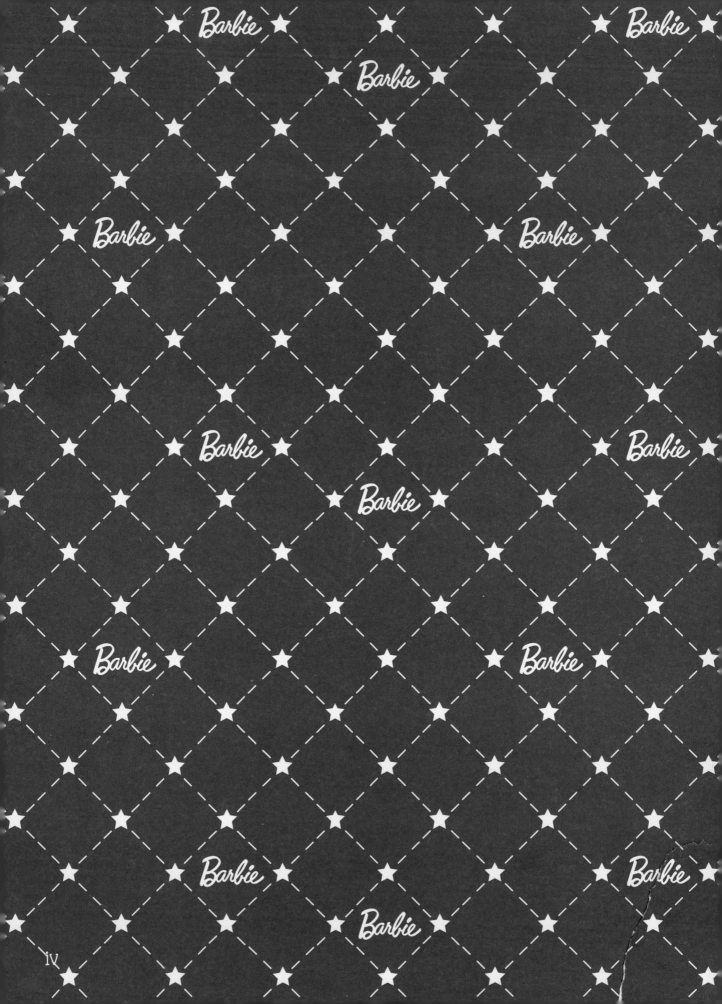

Barbie™

5-MINUTE STORIES

The Sister Collection

Published in the United States by Random House Children's Books, a division of Penguin Random House LLC, 1745 Broadway, New York, NY 10019. No part of this book may be reproduced or copied in any form without permission from the copyright owner. Random House and the colophon are registered trademarks of Penguin Random House LLC. The stories contained in this work were originally published separately and in slightly different form as *It's Sister Day!* adapted from *Happy Birthday, Barbie!,* copyright © 2014 Mattel; *Soccer Sisters* adapted from *Soccer All-Stars,* copyright © 2011 Mattel, Inc.; *Lacey's Busy Day* adapted from *I Can Be a Painter,* copyright © 2014 Mattel; *Sisters Onstage* adapted from *I Can Be an Actress,* copyright © 2011 Mattel, Inc.; *Chelsea Loses a Tooth* adapted from *The Loose Tooth,* copyright © 2015 Mattel; *Tawny's Big Jump* adapted from *I Can Be a Horse Rider,* copyright © 2010 Mattel, Inc.; *Skipper's Pet Sitters* adapted from *Skipper's Pet Hotel,* copyright © 2011 Mattel, Inc.; *Sisters Stick Together* adapted from *I Can Be a Martial Artist,* copyright © 2012 Mattel, Inc.; *A Flock of Sisters* adapted from *Sisters on Safari,* copyright © 2014 Mattel; *Tennis for Rey* adapted from *I Can Be a Tennis Player,* copyright © 2012 Mattel, Inc.; *The First Day of Summer* adapted from *I Can Be a Firefighter,* copyright © 2012 Mattel, Inc.

Visit us on the Web!
randomhousekids.com

Teachers and librarians, for a variety of teaching tools, visit us at RHTeachersLibrarians.com

ISBN 978-0-399-55209-0 (trade) — ISBN 978-0-399-55210-6 (ebook)

MANUFACTURED IN CHINA

10 9 8 7 6 5 4 3 2 1

Contents

It's Sister Day!

"Stacie! Skipper! Do you know what day it is?" Chelsea asked.

"Um, Saturday?" Stacie replied.

"No, it's Sister Day!" said Chelsea.

"What's Sister Day?" Skipper asked.

"I made it up," said Chelsea. "It's a day when you do fun things with your sisters. So let's do something fun!"

"I know what we can do," Skipper said. "Let's make Sister Day cards for each other."

The three girls used stickers, ribbon, and colored paper to make pretty cards for one another.

"Look, Lacey's helping!" said Stacie, laughing at the little Chihuahua.

Barbie walked in. "What's going on here?" she asked.

"It's Sister Day!" Chelsea announced. "Barbie, I made you a card."

"Sister Day, huh? I know something we can do together. Follow me!" Barbie said.

Chelsea, Stacie, and Skipper followed Barbie to her bedroom.

"I know a fun Sister Day game," Barbie said. "We can take turns doing each other's hair and makeup with blindfolds on!"

"No way!" Skipper said, then giggled.

"Come on. It will be fun," Stacie said, tying a scarf around her eyes.

"No peeking, Chelsea," Barbie told her little sister.

4

The sisters cracked up when they saw their crazy hair and makeup.

"You know what we need now?" Skipper asked. "Silly outfits!"

The girls raided Barble's closet and put together the most mixed-up outfits they could think of.

"Look, Blissa wants to get dressed up, too," Skipper said, pointing at their fluffy white cat.

Chelsea laughed and pointed at Barbie. "That is the best Sister Day outfit ever!"

"Can we go out for some Sister Day pizza next?" Stacie asked.

"Definitely!" said Skipper. "But only if we change our outfits first."

The sisters went out for pizza. When they got home, they changed into pajamas and brushed their teeth.

Chelsea sighed. "I wish Sister Day didn't have to end."

Barbie and Skipper looked at each other.

"Maybe it doesn't," Skipper said.

Barbie had an idea. "What would you say to a Sister Day slumber party?"

"I would say hooray!" Stacie cried, doing a karate kick to celebrate.

Chelsea's eyes got wide. "You mean I can stay up late with you?"

"Just a little bit late," said Barbie.

"Yay!" Chelsea said, doing her own karate kick. "Let's turn off all the lights. And put up some Sister Day decorations!"

Chelsea and Stacie ran to the closet and pulled out some colorful lights. They strung them all over Barbie's bedroom.

"It looks great," said Barbie. "And you know what? These decorations make me feel like dancing!"

The girls danced around the room. When they couldn't dance anymore, they flopped down on the rug.

"Snack time!" Barbie announced.

The girls settled down for some popcorn and drinks.

"I have an idea," said Skipper. "Let's tell spooky stories."

Barbie winked at Skipper and nodded toward Chelsea. "Nothing too spooky."

"I think we should tell sister stories," said Chelsea.

"What kind of sister stories?" Barbie asked.

"Like this one," Chelsea said. "Once, a girl and her sisters had Sister Day. They made crafts and put on silly outfits and danced and had a slumber party. And they stayed up all night!"

Barbie smiled. "Oh, they did, did they? They didn't sleep even a little bit?"

Chelsea shook her head. "Nope!"

"Well, look at Blissa," said Barbie. "She's very sleepy."

"That's Blissa. She's always sleepy," Chelsea said. "But I'm not."

Stacie grabbed a pillow. "Well, if you're not sleepy, you know what that means?"

"What?" asked Chelsea.

"Pillow fight!" Stacie cried. She playfully hit Chelsea on the head with her pillow.

"Watch your head!" teased Skipper, playfully hitting Barbie on the head with a pillow.

Taffy bounded in to see what all the noise was about. She wanted to be in on the fun, too. Taffy grabbed one end of Skipper's pillow and gave it a tug.

When the pillow fight ended, Chelsea yawned.

"Now I'm sleepy," she said. "But I don't want Sister Day to end!"

"It doesn't have to end," Barbie said.

The girls made a big sleep fort in the middle of the room. Then they happily snuggled down into the comfy pillows and blankets.

"I wish every day could be Sister Day," Chelsea said as she closed her eyes.

"But every day *is* Sister Day," Barbie said, "as long as we're together!"

Soccer Sisters

One afternoon, Barbie and Stacie met Ken at a park before soccer practice. They were going to run some drills with Stacie before the rest of her soccer teammates arrived.

"Hi, Ken!" said Stacie. "This is great. Thanks again for offering to help me. You and Barbie are talented soccer players."

"So are you, Stacie!" Barbie replied.

They started practicing right away. Barbie dribbled the ball and passed it to Stacie. The ball flew in the air toward her sister.

Stacie stopped the ball with her knees and let it drop to the ground. She gave a swift kick and scored a goal!

"Way to go, Stacie!" Barbie cheered.

"She shoots. She scores!" Stacie exclaimed. She raised her hands over her head and did a silly victory dance.

Barbie laughed at her funny sister. "You're such a goofball."

"It must run in the family," Stacie replied, grinning.

"But remember, when we're playing against a team, we need to practice good sportsmanship and be gracious when we score a goal," Barbie said.

"Thanks for the reminder, sis," Stacie replied.

The other players started to arrive. As the coach, Barbie wanted to see what the girls could do, so she divided the group into two teams.

Abby had the ball and dribbled it down the field. Then Stacie stole the ball. The only problem was that they were on the same team!

Barbie noticed that none of the players were talking to each other on the field. She called the girls over.

"Good footwork and great effort! But right now you're not playing as a team," she told them.

"She's right," said Ken. "Communication is important on a team."

"Just like in a family," Barbie said. "If my sisters and I don't communicate, things can get really mixed up."

"I know a fun game that can help us learn teamwork and communication," Barbie said. She and Ken set up an obstacle course on the field. Then Barbie paired up the girls and gave each pair a blindfold.

"One of you should put on the blindfold," Barbie instructed. "It's your partner's job to give directions to steer you through the obstacle course. You will really have to listen to each other!"

Stacie and Abby paired up.

"Okay, walk to your left . . . now lift your leg up and over . . . great!" Stacie told Abby.

After Abby got through the course, Stacie put on the blindfold.

"Great job, girls!" Barbie said. "You're really communicating!"

The team had learned how to talk to each other on the field. But at the next practice, a new problem came up: all the girls wanted the ball! They all wanted to score a goal.

"When you're on a team, everyone has to work together to win," Barbie said.

Then Barbie had an idea. "Come on," she told the team. "It's all of you—against Ken and me."

The girls smiled at each other—this was going to be a piece of cake! But beating them wasn't as easy as the girls had expected. Barbie and Ken had some pretty tricky moves.

After Barbie reminded the girls to work together to make a goal, they started to score.

"Woo-hoo!" The girls cheered and hugged one another.

That night, the team went out for pizza. Barbie and Ken smiled. The girls understood what it meant to work together.

Ken turned to Barbie. "I think they're finally ready for their first game."

"I'm excited and nervous at the same time!" Stacie exclaimed.

"Communicate, work together, and you'll do great!" Barbie promised. "And one more thing . . . have fun!"

The next day was game day. The other team was really fast on the field. Nobody on Stacie's team had scored a goal. Barbie could tell the girls were getting frustrated.

"You can do it!" Barbie cheered from the sidelines.

The girls relaxed a little bit. On the next play, one of the girls from the other team tried to pass the ball to her teammate, but Abby intercepted it. She dribbled down the field and then passed it to Stacie.

"I'm open!" Abby called out from the other side of Stacie. Stacie passed it back to her, and Abby made a goal!

Stacie's team was behind by only one point. In the last few seconds of the game, Stacie's teammate, Kirra, kicked the ball into the goal.

"Good job, Kirra!" exclaimed Stacie.

The team gave each other high fives.

Later, Stacie walked over to Barbie. "I can't believe we won our first game of the season!"

"You guys did a great job of communicating, working together, showing good sportsmanship, and having fun," Barbie said. "Just like a family."

The girls from the losing team walked up to Stacie and her teammates.

"Great game," they said with a smile as they shook each other's hands.

"Thanks," Stacie said. "We are a great family."

Lacey's Busy Day

"*Yip! Yip! Yip!*" barked Barbie's little Chihuahua, Lacey.

Barbie was in her dressing room at the movie studio. She was practicing her lines for her next movie.

"Hello, Lacey," Barbie said sweetly. "Do you want to sit on my lap?"

"*Yip! Yip!*" Lacey replied.

Barbie picked up Lacey.

"Here you go, Lacey," Barbie said.

Lacey settled down on Barbie's lap—but just for a minute. The puppy was full of energy. She started to tap Barbie's arm with her paw. Lacey wanted to play.

"Oh, I'm sorry, Lacey," said Barbie. "I wish I could play with you, but I have to read my lines out loud before we rehearse. I can't play right now."

Lacey jumped off Barbie's lap, and Barbie went back to her script. After a few minutes, Barbie heard a funny noise. She turned around in her chair.

"Lacey, no!" Barbie said. The little dog had found a shoe to chew on!

Barbie sighed. "What am I going to do with you?"

"Do with who?" Skipper asked, walking through the door.

"It's Lacey," Barbie said. "She wants to play, but I can't right now."

"I just stopped by to say hi on my way home," Skipper said. "I'll take her with me."

"Thanks, sis!" Barbie said. She picked up Lacey and kissed her on the head. "You'll be in good hands with Skipper."

Skipper brought Lacey back to the Dream House. Lacey soon found someone to play with—Sequin, the poodle.

"Aw, you guys look so cute together," Skipper said. Then she got an idea. "You know, I should paint a portrait of you for my art project! Keep playing. I've got to get changed."

Skipper changed into painting clothes and set up an art easel, pencils, and paint. She got busy sketching the playful dogs.

"Super cute," Skipper said. "But do you think you could hold still a little bit?"

Then Barbie's cat, Blissa, walked up to the dogs. She sat up straight and looked at Skipper.

"See? Blissa knows how to strike a pose," Skipper said.
Lacey and Sequin followed Blissa's lead. The three pets
posed perfectly while Skipper sketched them in pencil.
Then she began to paint.

"There. Almost done," Skipper said, stepping back to admire her work.

But the pets soon got restless. Lacey started to chase Sequin. Sequin knocked over the easel. Paint splashed on both of them!

"Oh no!" Skipper said. "Looks like it's bath time."

After her bath, Lacey walked outside in the sun to dry off. Chelsea was playing outside and scooped her up.

"Hi, Lacey," Chelsea said. "Want to play with me?"

"*Yip! Yip!*" Lacey barked. Then she licked Chelsea's cheek.

Chelsea giggled. She picked up Lacey's ball.

"Here, Lacey! Fetch!" she said.

Chelsea tossed the ball in the air. Lacey jumped up and hit it with her paws. Then Chelsea threw the ball again, and Lacey chased after it. Soon Lacey started to yawn.

"Oh, you need a nap, Lacey!" Chelsea said. "We can play again later."

Lacey settled into the soft grass for a nap. That's when Stacie walked by. She scooped up the Chihuahua.

"Lacey, I'm going to the pool," she said. "Want to come? My friends would love to see you."

"Yip! Yip!" Lacey barked.

Stacie got Lacey all ready for the pool. Lacey had her own sunglasses and floaties! Stacie and her friends helped Lacey doggie-paddle in the shallow end of the pool. Then Lacey started to yawn.

"Getting tired, Lacey?" Stacie asked. "Come on. Let's get you dried off."

After a long day working on the movie set, Barbie came home.

"Lacey, where are you?" Barbie called out. "I'm home. Now we can play!"

But Lacey didn't come when Barbie called.

"Lacey?" Barbie called again.

Barbie went into her bedroom and found Lacey sound asleep, curled up with her favorite toy. Barbie knelt down and patted her on the head.

"You're a tired puppy," she said. "You must have had a busy day."

In her dreams, Lacey was chasing Sequin, posing for Skipper, playing ball with Chelsea, and swimming with Stacie.

And in her dreams, Lacey answered Barbie. *"Yip!"*

Sisters Onstage

"What are you doing, Barbie?" Chelsea asked her big sister.

"Practicing my lines for my next movie," Barbie replied.

Chelsea sighed. "I wish I could be an actress, just like you."

Barbie thought for a minute. "You know, my friend Olivia is in a theater group," she said. "They're doing a play at the mall today. We should go see it. Maybe we can talk to her about giving you acting lessons."

"Yes! Let's do it!" Chelsea said.

When the sisters got to the mall, Barbie introduced Chelsea to Olivia.

"We're performing *The Princess and the Pea* today," Olivia said. "I'm playing the queen. And this is Benjamin. He's playing the prince."

"Sounds like fun!" Barbie said. "This is my little sister Chelsea. She's interested in acting."

Olivia smiled. "I hope you both enjoy the play! We're going onstage soon."

44

Barbie and Chelsea went to take their seats, but a few moments later, Olivia peeked out from behind the curtain and looked upset.

"I think something's wrong," Chelsea told Barbie. "Let's see if we can help!"

Chelsea and Barbie slipped backstage. Olivia looked panicked.

"Two of our actors have bad colds. They're not coming!" she said. "Do you think you two could take over their roles? We need someone to play the princess and her little sister."

Barbie and Chelsea looked at each other. "But we don't know the lines!" Barbie said.

"Well, Chelsea has just two lines," Olivia said. "And Barbie, you know the story. The other actors know their lines. You can answer them just like a princess would!"

Barbie and Chelsea remembered what they knew about the story: A stranger arrived at a castle claiming to be a princess. To test her, the queen put a pea under a pile of twenty mattresses! If the princess could feel the pea, it meant she passed the test and was truly a princess.

"Oh, please let's do it, Barbie!" Chelsea said. "We can't disappoint all the people out there."

Barbie smiled. "We'll do it! The show must go on, right?"

"Oh, thank you!" Olivia said. "Now let's get you two into costume."

Chelsea suddenly felt nervous. "There are a lot of people out there," she whispered to Barbie.

"Just relax and have fun onstage," Barbie told her. "You're going to be great!"

Soon Barbie and Chelsea were dressed in their beautiful princess gowns. Barbie gave Chelsea a hug.

"Don't worry. You were born to play my little sister!" Barbie said. "You know how to do that, right?"

Chelsea giggled. "Of course!"

"Girls, get ready for your scene," the director told them.

Barbie walked onstage. "It's a dark and stormy evening, and my sister and I need a place to sleep for the night!" Barbie said to the queen.

Then Chelsea walked out. "I should warn you. My sister can be very, very picky," she added.

"I will need the absolutely, positively, very, very, very, very best bed you have!" Barbie said. "Because I am a *princess*!"

The audience laughed.

Soon it was time for intermission. The stage crew needed some time to assemble the next set. Barbie and Chelsea decided to talk to the audience to make sure they were enjoying the show. And to sign some autographs, of course!

"Do you like the show?" Chelsea asked a boy.

"Yes! I can't wait for the next part!" he replied.

"Places, please!" the director called. Barbie and Chelsea went backstage.

"You and Chelsea are doing great!" the director said. "In the next scene, the queen will put the pea under the twenty mattresses. Barbie, you will need to climb up to the top of the mattresses and pretend to sleep."

"Got it!" Barbie replied.

In the following scene, Benjamin, who was playing the prince, walked out onstage. But he tripped and fell! Barbie thought quickly.

"Oh, Prince, I can see you've really fallen for me," Barbie said, helping Benjamin back to his feet. The audience laughed again.

Then it was time for the final scene. The queen and the prince came out.

"So you felt the pea?" the queen asked. "You really *are* a princess!"

Then Chelsea came out onstage and delivered the last line. "And they all lived happily ever after!"

The audience burst into applause.

"Time to take your bows, everyone!" the director said.

Barbie and Chelsea took their bows together.
Then Barbie gave her sister a hug.

"How did you like acting, Chelsea?" she asked.

"It was fun!" Chelsea said. "I just hope I can be
as good as you one day, Barbie!"

Chelsea Loses a Tooth

One day Chelsea was riding her bike with her favorite stuffed animal. She was pretending to be a princess on her way to a royal ball, but something didn't feel right.
   It was her tooth! It was wiggly!

When Chelsea got home, she changed and quickly told her sisters the exciting news!

"Barbie! Skipper! Stacie!" Chelsea called out. She ran through the house, trying to find her sisters.

"We're in the living room, Chelsea!" Barbie replied.

Chelsea ran to the living room. "Guess what? Guess what?"

"You're a magical princess?" Stacie teased.

"No!" Chelsea said. "My tooth is loose. My very first loose tooth!"

"Wow, your first loose tooth?" said Barbie.

"How does it fall out?" asked Chelsea. "Will the tooth fairy come?"

Skipper took out her phone. "Let's see if I can find some answers."

Stacie opened a book. "Maybe there will be some answers in here!"

"I have an idea," Barbie said. "Let's see if we can remember how we made our first loose tooth fall out."

"I think I was at my hip-hop dance class. I was dancing, and suddenly my tooth fell out," said Stacie.

Stacie and Barbie looked at each other and grinned.

"Dance party!" they said at the same time.

The sisters changed into their dance clothes. Chelsea
wore her ballet tutu.
    "Now one, two, three, twirl!" Stacie told her.
Chelsea twirled a lot. But her tooth didn't fall out!

The girls kept dancing.

"Skipper, how did you lose your first tooth?" Chelsea asked her sister.

Skipper thought. "I was jumping on a trampoline!"

"Let's try it!" said Barbie.

The sisters went outside and jumped on the trampoline.

They jumped . . . and jumped . . . and jumped.

"This is fun!" said Chelsea. "But I don't think my tooth is falling out."

"Keep jumping!" Stacie said.

So they jumped . . . and jumped . . . and jumped some more.

"Any luck yet?" Skipper asked.

Chelsea felt her tooth. "Not yet. And I'm getting a little dizzy."

The next day, Chelsea reminded her sisters that she still hadn't lost her tooth.

"I think you need a little break from this loose tooth," said Skipper.

"A musical break!" Barbie said with a wink to her sisters. The girls grabbed their instruments.

"I know a song we can sing," Chelsea said as she belted out her favorite song.

When the song was over, Chelsea had forgotten
about her tooth.
"I'm hungry," she said.
"Sounds good. I'm hungry, too," said Skipper.
The sisters went to the kitchen to have a snack.

While the sisters were enjoying a snack, Stacie turned to Barbie.

"Barbie, we never asked you. How did you lose your tooth?"

"By eating an apple!" Barbie replied.

Just then, Chelsea bit into her apple—and her tooth fell out!

"My tooth! My tooth!" she cheered.

Stacie gave her a high five. "Way to go, Chelsea! You lost your first tooth!"

"Can I put it under my pillow now?" Chelsea asked eagerly.

"You better wait until bedtime," Barbie told her.

That night, Barbie helped Chelsea put her tooth inside an envelope. Then Chelsea tucked it under her pillow.

"I don't think I'll be able to fall asleep tonight," Chelsea said. "I wonder what the tooth fairy will bring me."

"If you don't go to sleep, the tooth fairy won't come," Barbie reminded her. "Besides, you must be tired. Look at Blissa. She's so sleepy!"

Chelsea yawned. "Good night, Barbie."

"Sweet tooth-fairy dreams," Barbie whispered.

The next morning, Chelsea ran downstairs.

"The tooth fairy came!" she yelled as she showed everyone the shiny coin the tooth fairy had left her.

"Wow!" her sisters exclaimed.

Barbie hugged her little sister. "And I don't think any of us will forget how you lost your first tooth, Chelsea!"

Tawny's Big Jump

It was the morning of Stacie's big race, and she was a little nervous.

"What if I don't win?" she asked Barbie.

"As long as you do your best, you're a winner in my book!" Barbie replied. "I'm proud of you no matter what," she said, giving her sister a hug.

Stacie smiled and rode her horse behind the starting line.

Stacie rode her horse, Magic, with confidence. She remembered all the things she had learned in practice. At first, she fell behind, but soon she pulled ahead of the other racers!

"Go, Stacie!" Chelsea cheered from the stands as Stacie and Magic crossed the finish line.

Stacie congratulated all the other racers. They had been really tough competition!

Then she went over to her sisters with her trophy. They were all so proud of her!

"I knew you could do it," Barbie said.

A few weeks later, Barbie and Chelsea went to the stables. After seeing Stacie's race, Chelsea had started horseback riding lessons, too.

"Hi, Tawny! Hi, Starlight!" Chelsea said as she waved at the horses in the stable. This was her third horseback-riding lesson, and she was excited.

Chelsea was taking lessons with Starlight, a pretty white pony, while Barbie took Tawny out for practice.

"Do you want to help me get the horses ready?" Barbie asked.

"Yes, please!" said Chelsea.

They gave the horses some carrots and went to the tack room, where the saddles and bridles were kept. A poster on the wall caught Chelsea's eye.

"Look, Barbie!" she cried. "The Golden Saddle Show is next weekend. Isn't that where riders and their horses compete?"

Barbie nodded. "I'm going to enter with Tawny," she said. "We've been practicing for the jumping competition."

The sisters went back to the stables. Barbie helped
Chelsea saddle up Starlight.

"Are you and Tawny practicing jumping today?"
Chelsea asked.

"Yes, we still need a lot of practice," Barbie said,
tightening up the saddle. "There. You're all set, Chelsea.
Have a good lesson!"

Barbie rode Tawny to the jumping arena. Summer was practicing there, too.

"I'm a little nervous about practicing with Tawny today," Barbie told her friend. "She's a great show jumper, but she doesn't like jumping poles."

"Be confident, Barbie," Summer told her. "Like you told me, horses can pick up on their riders' feelings."

Barbie leaned toward her horse's head. "You can do it, Tawny," she whispered. Tawny pricked her ears and flew right over the next pole!

"We did it!" Barbie cheered.

During her lesson, Chelsea was going on a
countryside ride with her riding class. Skipper and Stacie
had offered to help out with the class. Chelsea waved
at Barbie as she rode by.

Barbie waved back. Then she kept practicing with
Tawny. She was getting more and more confident with
each jump!

A while later, Barbie heard the sound of pounding hooves. Starlight galloped out of the woods, whinnying with fright.

"Her saddle is empty!" Barbie gasped. "Chelsea must have fallen off in the woods!"

Barbie raced into the woods to find Chelsea. She flew through the trees, twisting and turning along the woodland path.

She quickly caught up to Chelsea's riding class.

"Chelsea tried to jump over a log," the instructor said. "Starlight didn't want to. She turned around and raced off, and Chelsea couldn't stop her."

Barbie and Tawny galloped away. Then Barbie heard a familiar voice.

"Help!" Chelsea cried.

"I'm on my way!" Barbie called out. She raced toward Chelsea's voice—and saw a huge log blocking the path!

"Come on, Tawny. We can do it," Barbie said as she rode toward the massive log. Tawny leaped into the air and cleared the huge log in a graceful arc.

"Well done, Tawny!" Barbie cried, patting the brave horse.

Barbie rode toward her sister's voice. "Where are you, Chelsea?"

"I'm down here," Chelsea replied. Barbie looked down and saw a steep bank. Chelsea was sitting on a ledge, waving up at her.

"Hold on, Chelsea!" Barbie said. "I'm coming."

Barbie carefully climbed down the bank and helped Chelsea up to the path. The little girl threw her arms around her sister and gave her a big hug.

Back at the stables, everybody was relieved to see them. Chelsea told everyone how Barbie and Tawny had saved her.

"I wanted to jump over a log, just like Barbie and Tawny," Chelsea said.

"Jumping takes practice," Barbie said. "From now on, always listen to your instructor, okay?"

"I will," Chelsea promised.

Barbie and Tawny practiced jumping all week. "We can do it, Tawny," she whispered.

Tawny gracefully jumped over every fence in the ring—even the biggest one!

Barbie and Tawny earned a blue ribbon for jumping. Chelsea cheered.

"That ribbon should be for being the Best Big Sister!" Chelsea said as she hugged Barbie. "I will never forget how you and Tawny saved me!"

Skipper's Pet Sitters

Skipper was busy looking online for a summer job. That's when her pug, Scrunchie, hopped onto the table in front of her. Scrunchie started pawing at the computer, trying to get Skipper's attention.

"What is it, girl?" Skipper asked. "Oh no! I lost track of time, and it's almost time to return Hudson to Ken!"

"*Yip!*" Scrunchie answered.

Hudson and Stacie were outside playing.

"Stacie, it's time to take Hudson home," Skipper called.

"I have to catch him first!" Stacie replied through laughter. "He might need a bath. . . . We've been running through some mud," she added.

Skipper and Barbie gave Hudson a quick bath. Skipper couldn't return him coated in mud!

Hudson was covered in white bubbles. Barbie laughed. "Hudson could be Sequin's younger brother!"

When Hudson was clean and dry, they brushed his fur.

The girls took the dogs outside and went to Ken's house.

"Skipper, thank you for watching my dog. And he smells so clean!" Ken said. "I was wondering if I could also hire you to watch him tonight."

"Sure!" Skipper said quickly.

When Ken left, Skipper turned to her sisters. "This is perfect! I've been looking for a summer job. I'm going to start a pet sitting business."

"Why don't we help you?" Barbie asked. "It can be a sister-run business."

"Thanks," Skipper said. "But I've got this!"

Skipper got busy. She came up with a name for her business: Skipper's Pet Sitters. She called and emailed everyone she knew who had a pet.

Then Skipper used some money she had saved up to buy supplies—toys, food, bowls, and some exercise pens.

"Wow, you're all set," Barbie said. "Are you sure you don't need any help?"

"I'm good," Skipper said. "This is going to be easy."

Soon the doorbell rang. It was Skipper's first customer, a cute gray kitten.

Then the doorbell rang again . . . and again . . . and again. Soon the house was filled with kittens, puppies, cats, and dogs.

"Um . . . Chelsea! Stacie! Barbie!" Skipper called out.

Chelsea came running first. She was happy to help with the kittens.

"Thanks, Chelsea," said Skipper. "I only need you for a few minutes. I'll be right back." Then she ran off to find Stacie.

Barbie heard meows coming from Chelsea's room.

"These kittens just won't listen!" Chelsea said.

"It looks like you've got your hands full," Barbie said. "I'll find Skipper."

Barbie went outside and saw Stacie covered in mud.
"Is everything okay?" Barbie asked.
"Absolutely!" Stacie said. "The dogs found a puddle, and we're all having fun. Skipper said she'd be back soon."
"Hmm," Barbie said. "I'll find her."

Barbie found Skipper by the pool, surfing the Web.

"Looks like maybe you could use some sister help after all," Barbie said.

Skipper nodded. "Definitely. A lot of people dropped off pets today, more than I was expecting. I'm looking at pet care sites to figure out what to do."

"Well, didn't you buy some exercise pens?" Barbie reminded her. "Maybe setting those up would help."

Skipper shut the laptop. "Barbie, that's it! Thanks, sis!"

Skipper came up with a plan—and she got her sisters to help.

"I'm going to set up two pens in the backyard," she said. "Barbie, can you please help Chelsea round up the cats and kittens? They can go in one pen."

"Of course!" Barbie said.

"And, Stacie, the dogs can go into the other pen while we set up an exercise and bathing area," Skipper said.

"Sounds good," Stacie said.

With the help of her sisters, they quickly set up the backyard. Soon all the pets were outside and having fun.

One by one, the sisters played with each pet, washed each dog, and brushed them all. By the time the sisters were done, Chelsea and Stacie were so tired that they fell asleep!

"Congratulations!" Barbie said. "It looks like Skipper's Pet Sitters is a big success."

"Thanks," Skipper said. "Except that—"

Before she could finish, a pet owner arrived to pick up her puppy. A stream of people stopped by to get their pets, and everyone was pleased to see the animals so happy and clean.

"What I was trying to tell you before is that Skipper's Pet Sitters is over," Skipper said.

"Oh no. Why?" Barbie asked.

Skipper smiled. "Because I'm changing the name to Four Sisters' Pet Sitters. I couldn't have done this without my sisters!"

Sisters Stick Together

Barbie and the other students in her martial arts class stretched. They did yoga poses to warm up for the martial arts moves they were about to perform.

Barbie loved the class. They were going to learn
defensive moves today. Barbie and her classmate Ben
demonstrated them for the class.

Skipper was taking a class. She hadn't been training as long as Barbie. During her class, Skipper had to practice throwing her partner. But Skipper kept falling down on the mat.

"I don't know if I'll ever be good at this," Skipper said. She looked down at the white belt around her waist. The color of the belt meant she was a beginner. "I'd love to earn my yellow belt someday."

"Just be patient, Skipper," Barbie told her. "I'll help you."
Skipper smiled. "Thanks! And I think I know another
talented sister who can help us."

Back home, Skipper found Stacie working on her laptop.

"So, Stacie, what do you say to some special sister martial arts practice sessions?" she asked. "You're a blue belt already. I bet you could teach me a few things. I really want to earn my yellow belt."

"Sounds like fun," Stacie said. "But I have to do my report first. Maybe I could do a report on you: 'Skipper Reaches for the Belt'!"

Barbie went into Chelsea's room to check on her littlest sister. Chelsea looked upset.

"What's wrong?" Barbie asked.

"Everyone knows how to do martial arts except me!" she said. "I don't want to be the only sister who doesn't know how."

"They have a children's class at the school," Barbie said. "I'll sign you up."

A few days later, Chelsea went to the children's martial arts class.

"I get to wear pajamas just like you, Barbie!" said Chelsea.

"These aren't pajamas!" Barbie laughed. "I'm wearing a martial arts uniform."

During Chelsea's class, Barbie and Skipper practiced sparring in the other room. Barbie showed Skipper how to do a roundhouse kick.

"This kind of kick gives your leg more power by swinging it around in a circle," Barbie explained.

Next they practiced throwing each other.
"Close your eyes and picture the perfect throw in your mind," Barbie said. "Then open your eyes and try your move."

After a few weeks of practice, the sisters went on a picnic together.

"I printed out my 'Skipper Reaches for the Belt' report," Stacie said. "Do you want to read it, Barbie?"

"Sure," Barbie said. "Skipper's goal of earning her yellow martial arts belt is getting closer."

Stacie smiled. "Just the other day I saw her throw Barbie on the mat in one swift, smooth move. If she keeps that up, she'll be sure to pass her yellow belt test."

"With Barbie helping and you and Chelsea cheering me on, I know I will!" Skipper said.

The next day Barbie and Skipper went to watch the children's class.

The girls were working with partners and practicing pinning them to the mat.

"Nice job, Chelsea!" Barbie said.

Afterward, Barbie and Skipper practiced for Skipper's yellow belt test. Finally the big moment came. With Barbie as her partner, Skipper showed the class how she could kick, throw, and tumble.

"Congratulations, Skipper," Ben said.

"Does that mean . . .?" Skipper began nervously.

"You've earned your yellow belt," Barbie said. "You've practiced very hard for this, Skipper. You deserve it."

"Thank you!" Skipper said. "I couldn't have done it without your help."

Barbie smiled. "I think you will make an excellent sensei someday!"

Barbie and her sisters were so excited! They were going on a vacation at an animal reserve.

"The reserve is a safe place for animals from all over the world," Stacie said to her sister Chelsea. "What kind of animals do you want to see?"

Chelsea thought for a minute. "Friendly ones."

Stacie laughed. "I'm sure there will be plenty of friendly animals here."

The sisters checked in to a hotel near the animal reserve. They decided they needed some accessories for their trip.

"These binoculars will help us get an up-close look at any animals we see," Skipper said.

"But, Skipper, won't you be busy taking pictures with your phone?" Barbie teased.

"Good point," Skipper said. "But these binoculars zoom in much better than my phone does!"

The next morning, the sisters went on a drive around the animal reserve. Skipper got ready with her tablet to record any animals they saw. She snapped an action picture of her sisters.

Barbie slowly drove down the road. Soon they saw their first animals.

"There you go, Chelsea," Barbie said. "Those koalas are friendly—just like you!"

Chelsea giggled. "Thanks, Barbie."

"I know!" Stacie said. "Let's play a game. Let's see which animals remind us of each other."

"Sounds like fun!" Barbie said.

The girls waved good-bye to the koalas.

Barbie drove on, and soon they found the perfect spot for a picnic.

Stacie started to unpack their picnic basket.

"Stacie, can you please pass the— Giraffe!" Skipper said with a confused look on her face.

"Pass the giraffe?" Stacie asked.

"It looks like we have a visitor," Barbie said.

"Stacie, that baby giraffe is like you," Skipper said. "She's so curious."

"I wonder what she's looking for," Stacie said with a grin. The baby giraffe galloped away on its long legs.

The girls finished their picnic and got back on the road. Barbie drove up to a pond filled with blue water. Chelsea grabbed the binoculars. "Look! Hippos!" Skipper typed into her phone.

"It says here that a group of hippos is called a pod," Skipper reported.

"What do you call a group of sisters?" Stacie asked. "A pod of sisters?"

"How about a flock of sisters just like that flock of birds over there?" asked Skipper.

"Wow, they're gorgeous!" Skipper said as they came upon some tropical birds.

"You know, Skipper, you remind me of a bird," said Barbie. "You're a free spirit."

"And your hair looks like colorful feathers," Stacie added.

They waved good-bye to the hippos and the birds.
"Can we look for more animals now?" Chelsea asked.
"We need to find an animal for you, Barbie."
Barbie drove around a bend, and the sisters gasped.
A small herd of elephants walked through the field.

"A group of elephants is called a herd," Skipper said.

"The elephants are one of my favorites," Barbie said. "Did you know that elephant families stick close together? Those two over there must be sisters!"

"That's like us!" Stacie said.

When they finished their tour of the reserve, the girls
posed for a picture.

"Smile, flock of sisters!" Skipper said.

"Or are we a pod of sisters?" asked Stacie.

"Or a herd of sisters?" Chelsea wondered.

"Well, I know what I would call this group of sisters,"
Barbie said.

"What?" her sisters asked.

Barbie smiled. "Absolutely amazing!"

Tennis for Rey

"Barbie, why are we making so many cupcakes, again?" Chelsea asked.

"We're having a bake sale to help the animal shelter," Barbie replied.

When all the cupcakes had been decorated, Barbie packed them up and took them to the bake sale. Everybody wanted to help the animals, and the cupcakes sold out!

The next day, Barbie took the money to Julie, the director of the animal shelter.

"Thanks, Barbie," Julie said. "This will help us buy food for the cats and dogs here."

Barbie knelt down to pet the dog Julie was walking.

"This is Rey. He's a greyhound," Julie said. Then she sighed. "We have so many animals right now. We're going to have to expand the shelter soon. But we need a lot of money for that."

Barbie was still thinking about Rey and the shelter animals when she picked up Chelsea and Skipper from their tennis lessons.

Barbie told Skipper about the animal shelter. "I wish I could think of a way to raise a lot of money to help them," she said.

"I know a way!" Skipper said. "We can compete in the doubles tennis tournament. The winner gets to choose a charity to donate the money to!"

Barbie frowned. "I love to play tennis. But I don't think I'm good enough for a tournament."

10th Annual Doubles
Charity Tennis Tournament

Prize money awarded to the charity of choice

"I can train you!" Skipper said. "Come on, Barbie. Let's do it!"

Barbie thought about Rey and all the dogs and cats like him that needed a home.

"All right," she said. "I'll do it!"

Skipper and Barbie started practicing the very next day. They used a ball machine to practice their strokes.

Skipper helped Barbie with her serve. "You've got to swing your racket across your body," Skipper coached. "And hit the ball nice and hard."

Barbie practiced her serve again . . . and again . . . and again.

"You're getting it, Barbie," Skipper said. "If you keep practicing, I think we might be able to win this!"

After practice, Barbie took Lacey with her and went to the animal shelter to invite Julie to the tournament. She found Teresa there, carrying a box of kittens.

"Teresa, do you volunteer, too?" Barbie asked.
"Kittens are my favorite," Teresa said. "I like to come here and play with them."
Lacey jumped right out of Barbie's arms and into the box with the kittens!

"I think Lacey likes playing with kittens, too," Barbie said with a laugh.

Then Julie walked in, and Barbie explained about the tournament.

"If Skipper and I win, the prize money will go to the shelter," Barbie said.

Julie smiled. "That's wonderful, Barbie. We just got two more dogs in today. I hope we never have to turn any dog away."

The day before the tournament, Skipper set up a doubles game with two of her friends.

"Now we'll see how we work as a team," Skipper said.

Barbie missed the first serve that came over the net.

"Next time don't move close to the net too soon," Skipper advised.

Barbie nodded. "Got it!"

On the day of the tournament, Barbie felt a little nervous. *Skipper's a great coach, but I hope I'm good enough that we can win and help the animal shelter!* thought Barbie.

Then she spotted Julie on the sidelines with Rey.

"I can't be nervous," she said out loud. "I've got to do this for Rey."

"Barbie, you serve first," Skipper said.

Barbie nodded. She swung her racket across her body. She hit the ball. It was a great serve!

Barbie and Skipper played hard. It was a tight match. After many tough games, Barbie and Skipper were a point away from winning.

It was Barbie's turn to serve again.

"Go, Barbie!" Chelsea and Stacie yelled from the stands.

"*Woof!*" Rey barked.

Barble grinned. She lifted her racket and threw the ball into the air.

Wham! She served hard—and her opponent missed the ball!

Skipper ran to her and hugged her. "We won!"

135

Barbie and Skipper had to beat two more teams to win the tournament. But Barbie's confidence was high. They won both matches—and earned the tournament trophy!

Afterward, Barbie met Julie and Rey on the sidelines and gave them the prize money.

"Barbie, this is a wonderful gift for the shelter," Julie said. "Thank you so much."

"I couldn't have done it without Skipper!" Barbie said. "She's a great tennis coach—but most of all, she's a great sister!"

The First Day
of Summer

"It's the first day of summer!" Barbie said to Skipper.

Skipper looked around. "You know what would get our summer started off right? Swimming and then a barbecue!"

Barbie smiled. "Let's do it!"

Just as the girls started listening to Skipper's "Best Summer Ever" playlist, Ken stopped by with Hudson.

"Hey, guys. Is it okay if I leave Hudson here for a few hours? I need someone to watch him for me," Ken said.

"Sure!" Barbie replied.

"Thanks so much!" said Ken as he left.

Barbie went back to listening to the playlist, but then she saw Skipper frown.

"What's the matter?" she asked.

"Well, you know I love Hudson. But he can be . . . well . . ."

"Energetic?" Barbie asked. "I know what you mean. But we'll keep an eye on him."

Then Skipper's stomach growled. "Let's start the barbecue!"

Barbie nodded. "You're right. I'm hungry, too. Let's grab the food from the kitchen."

"This is going to be the perfect spread," Skipper said as she and Barbie got the food. "We have beef burgers, veggie burgers, and hot dogs."

"And delicious grilled veggies and watermelon for dessert," Barbie added. "Sounds pretty perfect to me!"

Then Skipper saw something out of the corner of her eye. "Uh-oh," she said. "Hudson is going to . . ."

". . . jump!" Barbie said.

Splash! Hudson dove into the pool after a ball. He splashed water everywhere.

Then he jumped out of the pool and ran toward Skipper and Barbie.

"Aahhh!" Skipper cried as Hudson stood next to her and shook himself dry. "Thanks a lot, Hudson!"

"*Woof!*" Hudson barked.

"I'll go get you a towel," Barbie said.

While the girls ate their food, Hudson rushed to his food dish—and accidentally knocked into the table! A candle on the table fell into the bag of coal. A fire began to start.

Hudson ran and got Barbie.

"*Woof! Woof!*" Hudson barked.

"What is it, boy?" Barbie asked as she followed Hudson back to the grill. Then she realized what Hudson was trying to say.

"The bag of coals is on fire!" Skipper yelled.

"Stay calm," Barbie said. "First, let's step away from the fire. Then I am calling the fire department." She quickly dialed the fire department and explained what had happened.

Skipper remembered that they always kept a fire extinguisher by the pool house. She ran and grabbed it.

"Good thinking, Skipper!" Barbie said. She aimed the fire extinguisher at the flames. "This will keep the fire from spreading until the firefighters get here."

Soon they heard the sound of sirens, and a team of firefighters pulled up in their fire truck. Barbie explained the situation to them.

"You did the right thing by calling us right away," the fireman told the sisters. "It might have looked like a small fire, but fires can spread quickly."

"Well, we got an early warning thanks to Hudson," Barbie said. "And luckily Skipper remembered to grab the fire extinguisher."

The firefighters made sure the fire was completely extinguished.

"Most importantly, you remained calm," the firewoman said. "That is the most important fire safety rule."

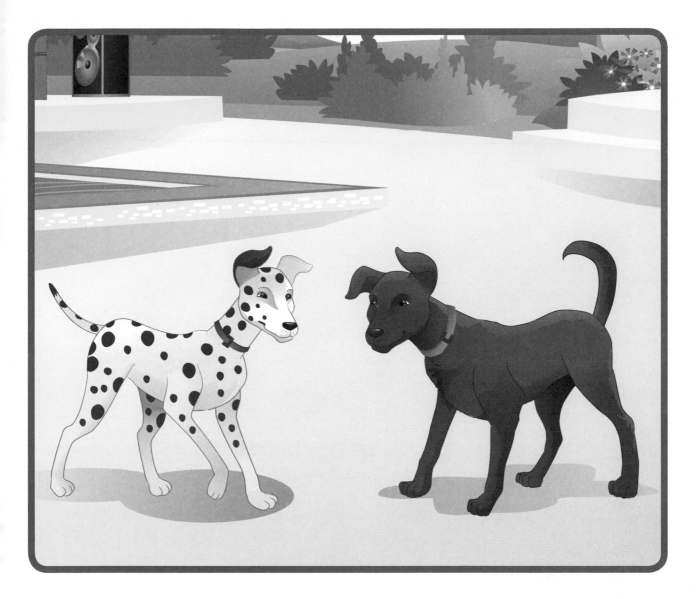

"Where's Hudson?" Skipper asked with a hint of worry.

"Don't worry. It looks like Hudson made a new friend," the firefighter replied.

"Hudson would make a good firehouse dog," the captain said. "At least our firehouse dog, Sparky, seems to think so."

A few weeks later, Skipper, Barbie, Ken, and Hudson visited the firehouse.

The firefighters gave them a tour, but most importantly, Hudson got to play with his new friend Sparky!

Barbie and Skipper looked at each other.

"Well that was a memorable first day of summer," Barbie said.

Skipper laughed. "That's for sure!"

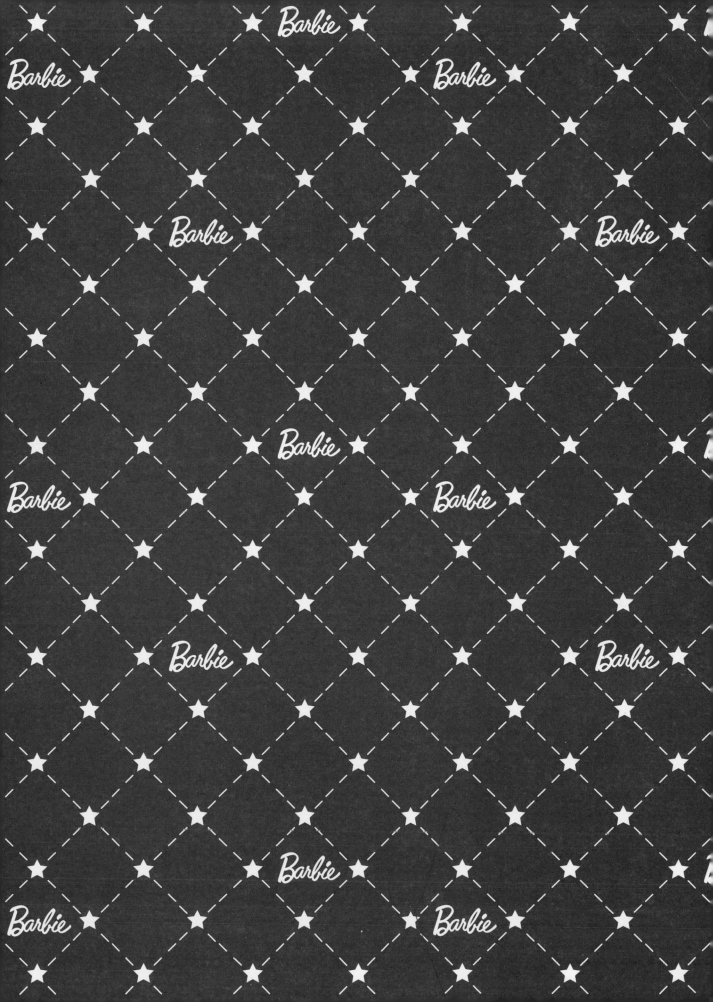

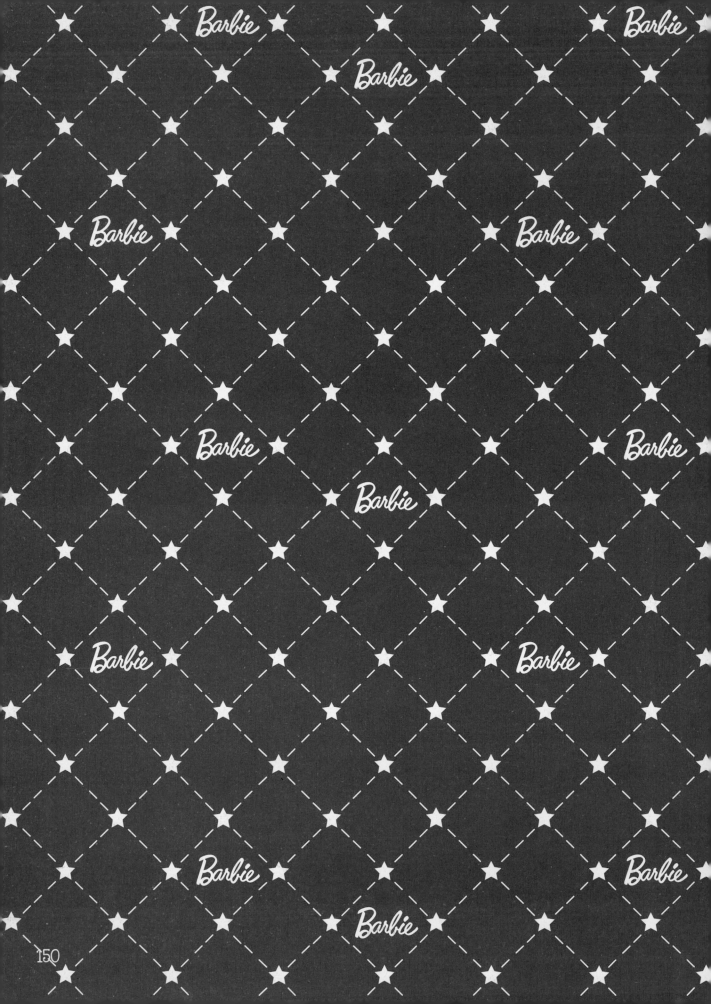